nickelodeon™

BUBBLE GUPPIES™

TIME FOR SCHOOL!

By Mary Tillworth

Based on the TV series *Bubble Guppies*, created by Robert Scull and Jonny Belt

Random House 🏠 New York

randomhouse.com/kids

ISBN: 978-0-449-81447-5

MANUFACTURED IN CHINA

10 9 8 7 6 5 4

3-D special effects and production: Red Bird Publishing Ltd., U.K.

Molly

"Hi! It's me, Molly. It's time for school! All my friends are waiting for me in my classroom!"

"Come on! Let's go see them!"

"Hi! I'm Gil. You know what my favorite thing about school is? Getting to be with all my friends!"

"There's our school up ahead. Come on!"

"Good morning, everyone!"
"Good morning, Mr. Grouper!"
"We can do so much in class today! Let's think about our favorite things to do in school."

Goby

"I'm Goby. My favorite part of school is hearing and telling stories at story time! I love making up stories about dragons!"

"I'm Deema! My favorite part of the day is playing store. What can I get for you, customer?"

"Hello. I'm Nonny. My favorite part of the school day is when we learn new and interesting facts. I know a lot of facts. For example, a school is a building where you learn new things, but a school is also what you call a group of fish. Interesting, right?"

"I'm Oona. My favorite part of school is playing with my friends. We make each other laugh, and if we have problems, we help each other out."

"This is Bubble Puppy! He likes to come to school, too. His favorite part of the day is when we're outside, where he can bury bones, play fetch, pop bubbles, and go on adventures!"

"Our class adopted Bubble Puppy from an animal shelter and built him a great doghouse. I like to take him for walks. But I have to hold on tight—Bubble Puppy can run really, really fast! *Whoooooaaa!*"

"And we love it when we get to go on a FIELD TRIP! Mr. Grouper takes us to the most *fin-tastic* places, where we always discover something new! That's what school is all about!"

"Thanks for visiting our *swim-sational* school!"